P9-BYR-245

For Leah and Ashley McDonough

—J. S.

For my daughters,
Caitilyn Laurel and Hallie Martine,
with all my love

—J. S.

Acknowledgments

Grateful acknowledgment is made to E. J. Brill, which granted permission to adapt Christiaan Hooykaas's story "A Balinese Folktale" from the book *India Antiqua: A Volume of Oriental Studies* (Leiden, Holland: E. J. Brill, 1947); to Dr. Jan Knappert for assistance in locating this tale; and to Sidhakarya for the frogs' song and advice on cultural details.

Library of Congress Cataloging-in-Publication Data
Sierra, Judy.
The dancing pig/Judy Sierra; illustrated by Jesse Sweetwater.
p. cm.
"Gulliver Books."
Summary: After being snatched by a terrible ogress who locks them in a trunk, two sisters are rescued by the animals that they have always treated with great kindness.
ISBN 0-15-201594-9
[1. Folklore–Indonesia–Bali Island.] I. Sweetwater, Jesse, ill.
II. Title.
PZ8.1.S573Ran 1999
398.2'095986'02
[E]–DC21 97-27983

First edition
F E D C B A

Printed in Singapore

The illustrations in this book were done with liquid acrylics, watercolor, and gouache on Arches watercolor paper.
The display type was set in Eva Antiqua.
The text type was set in Cloister Oldstyle.
Color separations by United Graphic Pte. Ltd., Singapore
Printed and bound by Tien Wah Press, Singapore
This book was printed on totally chlorine-free Nymolla Matte Art paper.
Production supervision by Stanley Redfern
Designed by Lydia D'moch

About the Story

The story of Klodan and Klonching is recorded in the folktale archive of the Gedong Kirtya Library in Singaraja, Bali. The basic plot of the tale is known virtually throughout the world: Children are left at home alone, and told not to open the door. A monster, or a predatory animal, comes knocking, having changed its voice to sound like the children's mother or caretaker. In most of these tales, the children are eaten and must either free themselves or be rescued from the belly of the beast. This Balinese tale is unique in that the twin girls are saved before they are eaten.

It's especially fitting that the Rangsasa is defeated by means of music and dance, since these arts are so important in Balinese life. *Rangsasa* is a regional variant of *Raksasa*, the name for an ogress in Hindu mythology. The Legong is a Balinese dance performed by slim, beautiful young girls, so it is particularly funny that a pig and a Rangsasa should dance it. The Balinese language is rich in onomatopoeic words for the noises made by animals, such as the frogs' *kek-kek* and *kung-kung*, the mouse's chewing sound, *kriyet-kriyet*, and the pig's *ngus, ngus.*

–J. S.

Pronunciation Guide

Klodan	kloh-DAHN
Klonching	klohn-CHING
kriyet	kree-YET
Legong	lay-GAHNG
ngus	noos
Rangsasa	rahng-SAH-sah
nangka	NAHNG-kah
tuung	toong
tuba-jenu	too-bah-JEH-noo
latengiu	lah-teng-IH-oo
gamelan	GAH-muh-lahn
ketug	kuh-TOOG

The Dancing Pig

JUDY SIERRA

ILLUSTRATED BY JESSE SWEETWATER

Gulliver Books
Harcourt Brace & Company
San Diego New York London

On the island of Bali, in a small house nestled between a dark forest and sunny rice fields, a woman lived with her twin daughters, Klodan and Klonching.

Every day the girls swept the house and the paths all around it. As they worked they were careful not to harm any living thing, no matter how small. When Klodan finished sweeping, she would always leave a bit of food on the ground beside a mouse hole, then wait for the little furry creature to nibble it—*kriyet, kriyet, kriyet.*

Just before sunset each day, the twins carried rice hulls and water to the family's pig. "How lonely you must be," Klonching would say, "with no one to keep you company." So the girls would dance the Legong for her while frogs made music. First the tree frogs began—*kek-kek, kek-kek;* then the bullfrogs joined in with their low *kung! kung!* All together they sang:

kek-kek, kung! kung!
kek-kek, kung! kung!
kek-kek kung! kek!

This made the pig grunt happily—
ngus, ngus, ngus.

In the forest shadows, someone was hiding and watching. It was the Rangsasa, an ogress who lived beyond the graveyard. The Rangsasa had round eyes to see everything, and big ears to hear everything, and long, sharp fingernails to reach out and grab little ones like Klodan and Klonching. She wanted so badly to seize the twins as they danced, but she didn't dare as long as their mother was nearby.

One morning the girls' mother sat down with them. "Our money is nearly gone," she said with a sigh, "so I must go to market and sell *nangka* seeds. Promise me that while I am away you will stay inside the house and keep the doors and windows locked, in case the Rangsasa should come."

"Take us with you to market," the twins begged.

"It is too far," their mother told them. "You must stay here. When I return I will knock three times and say, 'Klodan, Klonching. It's your mother. Let me in.' Only then may you open the door."

The Rangsasa watched and listened that day, and the next day, and the next. Each day the girls' mother arrived home just before sunset. In the afternoon of the fourth day, the ogress herself stepped through the gate and knocked at the door—*tok, tok, tok.* Her voice was low and rough: "Kloodoon, Kloonchoong. Oots yoor moother. Loot moo oon."

"That's not our mother's voice!" Klonching cried out.

The Rangsasa went back outside the gate. She practiced making her voice very sweet. Then she knocked at the door again–*tok, tok, tok.* "Kleedeen, Kleencheeng. Eets yeer meether. Leet mee een."

"Go away!" shouted Klodan, "You are not our mother!"

The Rangsasa raced home. She cooked up a potion of *tuung* fruit and *tuba-jenu* root and the scorched bark of a *latengiu* tree. She lifted the pot to her lips and poured the hot mixture down her throat. Her insides started to itch. Her belly began to burn. She jumped up and down chanting, "Klodan, Klonching, Klodan, Klonching," until she sounded exactly like the girls' mother. Then she hurried back to the house and knocked at the door—*tok, tok, tok.* "Klodan, Klonching. It's your mother. Let me in."

"Mother!" the twins cried. "At last you're home!" And they unlocked the door and rushed outside. The Rangsasa grabbed Klodan with her right hand and Klonching with her left. Clutching the twins tightly with her fingernails, she carried them to her house. She pushed the two girls into a wooden chest, closed the lid, and tied it with a rope. Then she stoked the cooking fire and waited for it to blaze.

When the twins' mother arrived home, she found the door of the house open. "Klodan! Klonching! You naughty girls!" she shouted. "Where are you?" She lit a lantern and ran to all the corners of the compound, frantically calling her daughters' names. She was surprised to see the pig standing up on her hind legs. She was even more surprised when the animal spoke to her.

"The Rangsasa has stolen Klodan and Klonching," said the pig. "But if you promise to do everything I say, my friends and I can bring them home safely."

"I will do anything," said the mother.

"Take me to your house," said the pig, "and dress me in your best sarong and finest jewelry."

The mother did as she was told. She stretched a sarong around the pig's middle and tied it with a sash.

"I need two dance fans," the pig told her, and the mother got those as well. She tucked a fresh flower behind each of the animal's ears.

A mouse appeared, carrying a tiny torch. Then the frogs arrived. One tree frog held a tiny flute, and the other a pair of cymbals. A big bullfrog carried a gong, while a smaller one toted a drum.

The mother watched this strange procession march out the gate of the compound. The mouse led the way, quiet and watchful, and the frogs and the pig tiptoed along behind her. On they walked, until they reached a clearing not far from the Rangsasa's house. Then the pig hid behind a tree, and the frogs began to play and sing: *kek-kek, kung! kung! kek-kek, kung! kung! kek-kek kung! kek!*

The sound soon reached the Rangsasa's ears. It charmed her out of her house and drew her into the clearing. "Wah!" she exclaimed when she saw the frogs. "I have lived a long time, but never have I seen such a tiny gamelan orchestra!"

She was even more surprised when a pig stepped into the torchlight and began to dance the Legong. The pig swayed and turned gracefully, flicking her fans to the rhythm of the music as her eyes flashed left, then right.

The Legong is a dance for two, and soon the Rangsasa felt herself pulled along by the frogs' playing. The pig handed her a fan, and together they circled and danced.

As soon as the Rangsasa began to dance, the mouse scurried inside her house and climbed onto the wooden chest. "Don't worry, Klodan and Klonching," the mouse chirped, and she began to chew the rope—*kriyet, kriyet, kriyet, kriyet.* "Now, push!" said the mouse. Klodan and Klonching lifted the lid and stepped out to freedom.

"Take as much of the Rangsasa's treasure as you can carry," the mouse told the girls. "She will not need it anymore." While the twins gathered jewels and gold, the mouse nudged a red-hot ember from the Rangsasa's cooking fire onto the floor.

The twins followed the mouse, their hearts beating quickly—*ketug, ketug, ketug*—so afraid that the Rangsasa would see them. But the frogs' music held her in its spell. On and on they played and sang, while the pig and the ogress danced the Legong.

Suddenly the Rangsasa smelled smoke. She ran back inside her house, just in time to watch the four walls go up in flames all around her.

Klodan and Klonching carried the Rangsasa's treasures to their mother. Never again did she have to sell fruit at the market or leave the twins alone. In the evenings the three of them always shared their food with the pig and the mouse, while the frogs serenaded them: *kek-kek, kung! kung! kek-kek, kung! kung! kek-kek kung! kek!!*

But the pig never danced again. She was content to watch the twins as she grunted happily—*ngus, ngus, ngus.*